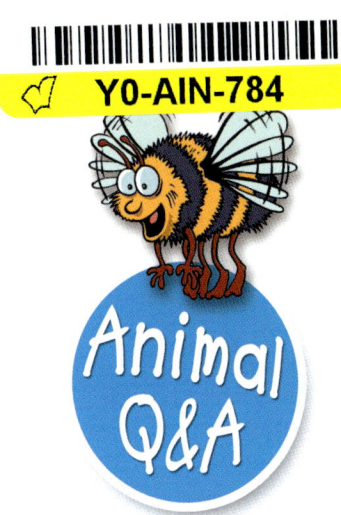

BUGS

Lucy Dowling

New York

Published in 2015 by Windmill Books, An Imprint of Rosen Publishing
29 East 21st Street, New York, NY 10010

Copyright © 2015 by Miles Kelly Publishing Ltd/Windmill Books, An Imprint of Rosen Publishing

All rights reserved. No part of this book may be reproduced in any form without permission in writing from the publisher, except by a reviewer.

US Editor: Joshua Shadowens
Publishing Director: Belinda Gallagher
Creative Director: Jo Cowan
Assistant Editor: Lucy Dowling
Volume Design: Debbie Oatley
Cover Designer: Jo Cowan
Indexer: Hilary Bird
Production Manager: Elizabeth Collins
Reprographics: Stephan Davis, Thom Allaway, Lorraine King

All artwork from the Miles Kelly Artwork Bank
Cover: vnlit/Shutterstock.com

Library of Congress Cataloging-in-Publication Data

Dowling, Lucy, author.
 Bugs / by Lucy Dowling.
     pages cm. — (Animal Q & A)
 Include index.
 ISBN 978-1-4777-9186-8 (library binding) — ISBN 978-1-4777-9187-5 (pbk.) —
 ISBN 978-1-4777-9188-2 (6-pack)
 1. Insects—Miscellanea—Juvenile literature. 2. Children's questions and answers. I. Title.
 QL467.2.D69 2015
 595.7—dc23
                                        2014001237

Manufactured in the United States of America

CPSIA Compliance Information: Batch #WS14WM: For Further Information contact Windmill Books, New York, New York at 1-866-478-0556

Contents

Are all bugs insects?	4
How many wings does an insect have?	5
Do insects have skeletons?	5
Where do butterflies come from?	6
How far can a flea jump?	7
Which butterfly flies the highest?	7
Why are butterflies brightly colored?	8
Where do cockroaches live?	9
Can insects walk on water?	9
Why do bees make honey?	10
How many times can a bee sting you?	11
Why do bees have a queen?	11
Why do spiders make silk?	12
Can spiders spit?	12
Do spiders have fangs?	13
Which insect is a flying hunter?	14
Do insects like to pray?	15
Can insects spread disease?	15

Why are scorpions' tails so deadly?	16
Which beetle carries a spray gun?	17
What is the deadliest spider?	17
Why do ladybugs have spots?	18
Which insect glows at night?	19
Can beetles dive?	19
Why do ants cut up leaves?	20
Which spider looks like a crab?	20
Why do moths like the moonlight?	21
Do earwigs really live in ears?	22
Glossary	23
Further Reading	23
Index	24
Websites	24

Are all bugs insects?

Insects are the largest of all the animal groups. There are millions of different kinds that live almost everywhere in the world. Not all bugs are insects. Spiders belong to a group called arachnids, and millipedes are in yet another group called myriapods.

Garden spider is an arachnid

Pill millipede is a myriapod

Ladybug is an insect

Dinner date!

Breeding time is very dangerous for the praying mantis. After mating, the female may eat the male.

How many wings does an insect have?

Most insects have two pairs of wings, and they use them to fly from place to place. A large moth flaps its wings once or twice each second, while some tiny flies flap their wings almost 1,000 times each second.

Do insects have skeletons?

Insects do not have a bony skeleton inside their bodies like we do. Instead, their bodies are covered by a series of horny plates. This is called an exoskeleton.

Moth

Look

Have a look in your garden, under rocks and in the soil. How many different insects can you find?

Where do butterflies come from?

① Caterpillar hatches from an egg

Butterflies start off life as caterpillars — wriggly grubs that hatch from eggs. Caterpillars eat lots of leaves, and when they are big enough, they attach themselves to twigs. They form hard shells called pupas. Inside the pupa, the caterpillar changes into a butterfly. When the butterfly is fully formed, it breaks out of its pupa.

② Pupa is formed

③ Butterfly breaks out of its pupa

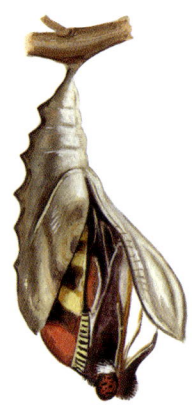

Fast mover!
The green tiger beetle is a fast-moving hunter that races over open ground. It chases smaller creatures such as ants, woodlice, worms and spiders.

④ Butterfly flies away

Peacock butterfly

Paint

Fold some paper in half. Open it up and paint two butterfly wings on one side. Fold it again and open it up to see all of the butterfly.

How far can a flea jump?

Fleas can jump a very long distance for their body size. These tiny insects measure just 0.08 to 0.12 inches (2–3 mm) in length. They can jump over 11.8 inches (30 cm), which is more than 100 times their body size.

Flea

Which butterfly flies the highest?

One of the strongest insect fliers is the Apollo butterfly. It can fly high over hills and even mountains, then it rests on a rock or flower in the sunshine.

Why are butterflies brightly colored?

Like many butterflies, the monarch butterfly has bright, bold colors on its wings. These warn other animals, such as birds and lizards, that it tastes horrible and is not good for them to eat.

Tasty treats!

Animal droppings are delicious to many kinds of insects. Various beetles lay their eggs in dung. The young insects then hatch out and eat it.

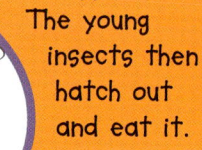

Where do cockroaches live?

Just about everywhere! Cockroaches are beetles that run quickly across the ground. They have low, flat bodies and can dart into small spaces under logs, stones and bricks. They can also hide in cupboards, furniture and beds!

Cockroach

Think
Write a list of any fast-running animals that you can think of.

Can insects walk on water?

Some insects can. The water strider has a slim, light body with long, wide legs, which allow it to glide across the surface of the water.

Monarch butterfly

Why do bees make honey?

Bees make sweet, sticky honey packed with energy. Wild bees make honey to feed themselves and their growing young, which are called larvae. Lots of animals eat honey, including humans, who keep honeybees in nests called hives so that the honey is easier to collect.

Honeybees

How many times can a bee sting you?

A bee can only sting once in its whole lifetime. After a bee jabs its sting into an enemy, the sting stays in its victim. As the bee flies away, the rear part of its body tears off and the bee soon dies.

Sting

Yummy!
Ants get food from insects called aphids. When an ant strokes an aphid, it oozes a drop of liquid called honeydew, which the ant then drinks.

Taste
Ask an adult if you can taste some honey. See if you think it tastes sweet and sticky, too.

Why do bees have a queen?

The queen bee lays all of the eggs, from which young bees hatch. Without her, there would be no other bees. Worker bees look after the queen and the eggs.

Why do spiders make silk?

Spiders make very thin, fine threads called silk. Some spiders use their silk to make webs to catch their prey. Other spiders wrap up their victims in silk to stop them from escaping. Female spiders make silk bags called cocoons and lay their eggs in them.

Can spiders spit?

The spitting spider can. It feeds on mosquitoes, moths and flies. When it spots its prey, it spits a sticky silk thread over it. This stops the victim from moving, so the spider can eat it.

Fly stuck in web

Find

See if you can find a spider's web. Look in the corners of windows, in garages and in sheds.

Spider on its web

Do spiders have fangs?

Spiders have sharp fangs in their jaws, which they use to grab and bite their prey. The fangs inject a venom to kill the victim. The spider then eats its food by sucking out the body juices.

Crowded house!

A wasps' nest may have about 2,000 wasps in it, but a termite colony may have over five million termites.

Which insect is a flying hunter?

Dragonflies are fierce flying hunters. Their huge eyes spot tiny prey such as midges and mayflies. They dash through the air and use their legs to catch their victims. Then they fly back to their perch to eat their meal.

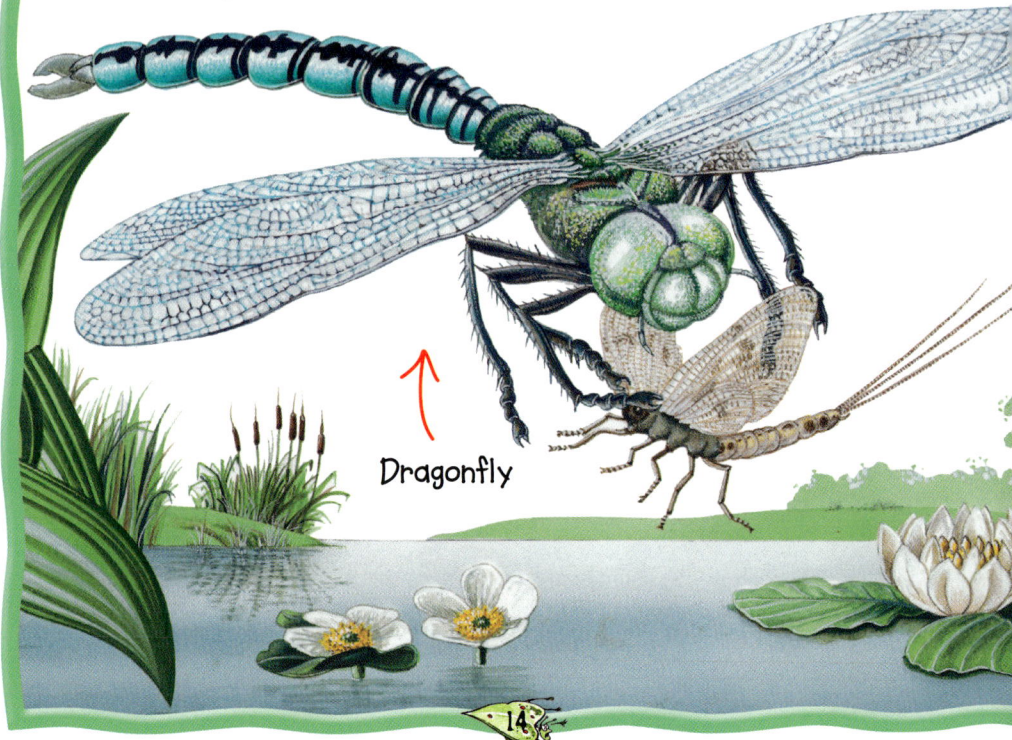

Dragonfly

Do insects like to pray?

The praying mantis is named because its front legs are folded, as if it is praying. In fact, it is waiting to grab some food. It waits for a fly or moth to come near, then SNAP! It grabs the victim very quickly with its front legs.

Praying mantis

Remember

Can you remember what dragonflies like to eat? Read these pages again to find out.

Can insects spread disease?

Many insects spread germs and disease. The mosquito is one of the deadliest. In hotter parts of the world, when it bites people to suck their blood, it may pass on a terrible illness such as malaria or yellow fever.

Playing dead!

When in danger, the click beetle falls onto its back and pretends to be dead. When the danger has gone, it arches its body and then straightens out with a jerk and a click!

Why are scorpions' tails so deadly?

Scorpions have poisonous stings at the end of their tails. They use them to attack their victims. Scorpions may also wave their tails at enemies to warn them that, unless they go away, they will sting them to death!

Scorpion

Which beetle carries a spray gun?

The bombardier beetle squirts out a spray of smelly liquid from its rear end, almost like a small spray gun! This startles and stings an attacker and gives the beetle time to escape.

Discover
Spiders and scorpions belong to the same family group. Try and find out what the group is called.

Scary spiders!
The name tarantula was first given to a type of wolf spider from Europe. Tarantulas are the biggest type of spider and live in hot parts of the world.

What is the deadliest spider?

Black widow spiders are the most feared and dangerous of all spiders. They are small, shiny and black, and they have a poisonous bite that can kill people. After mating, the female black widow spider may eat the male.

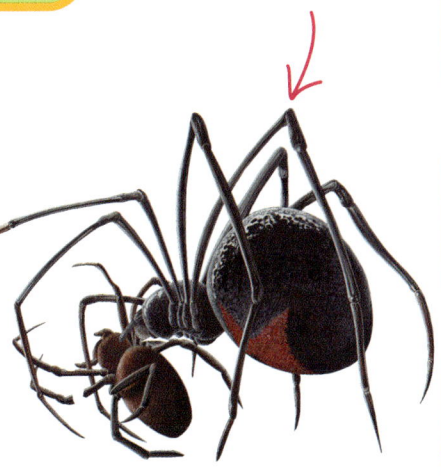

Black widow spider

Why do ladybugs have spots?

Ladybugs have bright pink, yellow or red bodies that are covered in black spots. These bright colors and spots tell other animals not to eat them, as they don't taste very nice.

Ladybug

Which insect glows at night?

Fireflies are not flies but a type of beetle. They produce a green or yellow light from their stomachs to attract a partner. Fireflies live on plants and trees during the day and are only active at night.

Think
Can you name any other insects or animals that have spots?

Firefly →

Sticking around!
Stick and leaf insects look exactly like sticks and leaves. When the wind blows, they rock and sway in the breeze like real twigs and leaves.

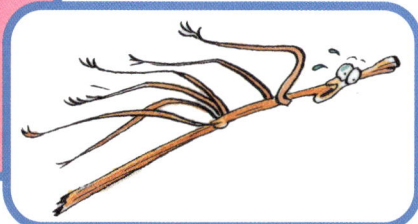

Can beetles dive?
Yes, beetles can dive. The great diving beetle lives in ponds and lakes and is a fast and fierce hunter. It uses its legs like paddles to dive through the water and catch its food.

Why do ants cut up leaves?

Leaf-cutter ants cut up small sections of leaves to take back to their nests. The ants then carry the leaves back to a special 'ant' garden where they are stored and used as food for the ants.

Which spider looks like a crab?

Crab spiders look like small crabs with wide bodies and curved legs. They sit on flowers and lie in wait for small insects to grab and eat.

Think

Do you know of any other animals that become active after dark?

Why do moths like the moonlight?

Most moths, such as the Indian moon moth, like moonlight. They use it to search for plant juices such as nectar in flowers. By day they rest in cracks in rocks or among leaves.

Moon moth

Tough bug!
The young of the cranefly or 'daddy long-legs' is called a leather jacket after its tough skin.

Leaf-cutter ants

Do earwigs really live in ears?

Earwigs don't really crawl into ears or hide in wigs. But they do like dark, damp corners. At night they come out to feed on flower petals, one of their favorite foods.

Earwig

Discover
Try to find out what other animals migrate when the weather gets colder.

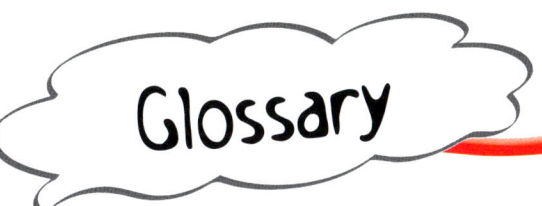

Glossary

arachnids (uh-RAK-nids) A type of animal that includes spiders and ticks.

cicada (suh-KAY-duh) A large insect that makes loud sounds.

cocoons (kuh-KOONS) A soft outer covering that some bugs put around themselves as they grow.

exoskeleton (ek-soh-SKEH-leh-tun) The hard covering on the outside of an animal's body that holds and guards the soft insides.

honeydew (HUH-nee-doo) Sweet matter produced by aphids, which are bugs.

larvae (LAHR-vee) Insects in the early life stage in which they have a wormlike form.

myriapods (MIR-ee-oh-pods) Any of several arthropods, such as the centipede or millipede, having segmented bodies, one pair of antennae, and at least nine pairs of legs.

venom (VEH-num) A poison passed by one animal into another through a bite or a sting.

Further Reading

Brookes, Olivia. *Ask a Bug*. Ask. New York: PowerKids Press, 2009.

Roza, Greg. *Beastly Beetles*. World of Bugs. New York: Gareth Stevens, 2011.

Wood, Alix. *Yucky Animals in the Yard*. Earth's Grossest Animals. New York: Windmill Books, 2014.

Index

A
ant(s), 6, 11, 20
arachnids, 4

B
bee(s), 10–11
beetles, 6, 8–9, 15, 17, 19

C
caterpillar(s), 6
cockroaches, 9
cocoons, 12

D
disease, 15
dragonflies, 14

E
earwigs, 22
eggs, 6, 8, 11–12
exoskeleton, 5

F
fireflies, 19
flea, 7
flower(s), 7, 20–22
food, 11, 13, 15, 19–20, 22

G
germs, 15

H
hives, 10
honey, 10

L
ladybugs, 18
larvae, 10
lizards, 8

M
millipedes, 4

mosquito(es), 12, 15
moths, 5, 12, 15, 21

N
nest(s), 10, 13, 20

P
plant(s), 19, 21
ponds, 19
praying mantis, 5, 15
pupa(s), 6

Q
queen, 11

S
scorpions, 16
stings, 11, 16

W
webs, 12

For web resources related to the subject of this book, go to:
www.windmillbooks.com/weblinks and select this book's title.

4-13-15